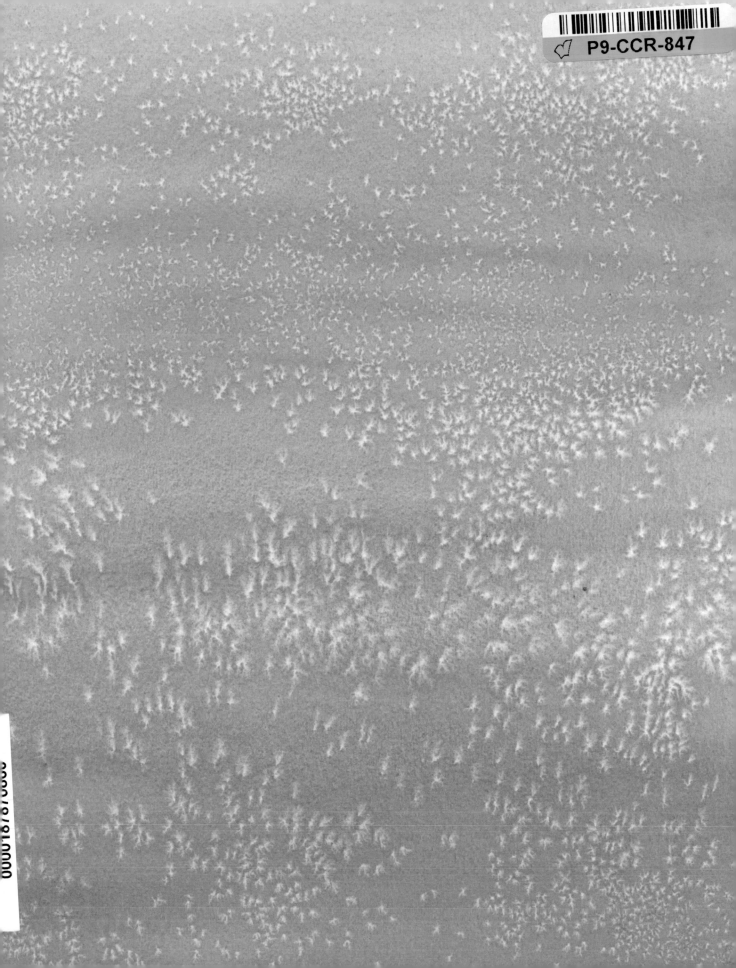

CHIA and the FOX MAN

An Alaskan Dena'ina Fable

Retold by Barbara J. Atwater and Ethan J. Atwater

Illustrated by Mindy Dwyer

ALASKA
NORTHWEST
BOOKS®

My name is Chia. I am an orphan. My parents died when I was young, but I still remember sukdu time in the evenings. The stories they told taught me lessons about life, about how to behave and do what is right.

Well, one day I learned about that—how sometimes it can be hard to do the right thing. I will tell you my sukdu.

sukdu (SOOK du): story

With no family to care for me, I went to live in the qenq'a of a rich man in our village. Nestled into a hillside above a lake, our village looked safe and snug, but things were not good there.

qenq'a (KUNK ah): house

Even though it was early spring, winter lingered.

Our hunters went out every day, but returned with nothing.

We ice fished, but the hooks came up empty.

Our food caches and cellars were bare.

And so, di'eshchin: I was hungry.

di'eshchin (dee USHK een): I was hungry.

Even with my hunger, I had chores to do.

I carried firewood to keep us warm.

I hauled water from the lake in birch bark buckets.

I fed the dogs a salmon bone with bits of dried fish on it.

The dogs howled mournfully at night,
reminding us of how hungry we were.

After a long day filled with many chores and no food,
I was tired. I crawled into bed and fell quickly asleep.
Suddenly, I was awakened by a loud yell.

"Ezhi'i, Chia! it is cold!" cried the rich man. "Fix the door!"

ezhi'i (ee zhi EE): it is very cold

A storm had blown it open. Wind and snow were rushing into the qenq'a. I closed the door, fixed the latch, and went back to sleep.

Soon, the rich man's voice woke me again. "Ezhi'i, Chia! The door!" A second time I fixed the latch and wearily went back to bed.

A third time the rich man's shouts woke me. "Ezhi'i, Chia! Fix the door!"

I sat up and stared at the open doorway. Something was happening. This time I pulled on my boots, my parka, and my mittens, and I ran outside.

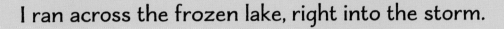

I ran across the frozen lake, right into the storm.

I ran through the forest, directly into the wind.
I ran up the mountainside, straight into the blowing snow!

tink

tink

tink

High up on the mountain I heard something. At first it was
faint, but it grew louder and louder as I neared the glacier.

As I got closer I saw someone. It was Fox Man! He was chopping away at the glacier with his duguli. Chips of ice got caught up by the wind and carried straight down to our village.

duguli (DOO gu lee): axe

I watched in wonder, trying to decide what to do. Finally, I had an idea.

tink

tink

tink

I snuck up behind
Fox Man. He didn't
see me—the clouds
of snow hid my
sneaking figure.

He didn't hear me—
the stormy wind
drowned out my
creeping footsteps.

He did not know
I was coming. He just
kept chopping away
at the glacier with
his duguli.

I crept up closer and closer until I was right behind him.
He raised the duguli up over his head and then...

I jerked it out of his hand. Fox Man went sprawling into the snow. I ran away as fast as I could!

Down the mountain.

Through the forest.

Across the lake. And back to the qenq'a. I fastened the door latch and tucked the duguli under my sleeping mat.

No more wind. No more snow. Now the rich man couldn't complain anymore.

Finally, I would be able to sleep. But my sleep was interrupted again. Fox Man was in my dreams!

I ran down the mountain and he was the glacier blowing snow at me.

I ran through the forest and he was the trees tangling me in branches.

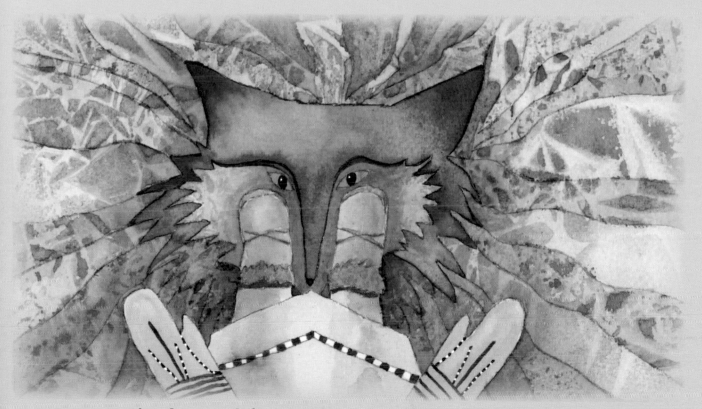

I ran across the frozen lake and he was the ice cracking beneath me.

I awoke in a sweat to find Fox Man standing beside my bed. "Please don't hurt me!" I cried.

He tilted his head to the side. "Chia, dnazeht'in. You stole from me."

dnazeht'in (dnah ZEET een): you stole from me

This was true, but strangely he did not seem angry. I stammered, "You were causing the storm which was making our lives more difficult."

Fox Man just stared at me. "I need my duguli back."

I stood up in a rush. "I'm tired and hungry and I needed the storm to stop!"

Fox Man turned his head toward the door and spoke softly, "I have work to do."

Fox Man looked me in the eye and I realized what I had done was wrong. "I am sorry. I did steal your duguli," I said, pulling it out and handing it to him. "I was wrong."

Fox Man took the duguli and said, "Chin'an, Chia. Things will now get better for you."

chin'an (chi NUN): thank you

I watched him walk around the qenq'a,
dragging his duguli behind him.

He made a circle in the snow all the way
around it and then disappeared into the night.

I went inside, fastened the latch,
and fell into an exhausted asleep.
This time Fox Man did not chase me in my dreams.

When I awoke, all was quiet. The wind had stopped
howling. The snow had stopped falling. The rich man
was sleeping quietly.

It was just as Fox Man had promised. Things got better.

The weather warmed up. The hunters returned with rabbit and spruce hen. The fish started biting again.

We were not so hungry anymore.

Our village was a happier place.
Even the rich man was kinder to me.

I am still Chia. I still live in the home of the rich man.
But my life is better, just as Fox Man promised.

I have not seen Fox Man since that night.
But sometimes I see a faint outline of his circle
around the qenq'a.

Sometimes I think I see him in the forest. And there are times when I can almost hear his duguli chopping away at the glacier.

On that night when I stole from Fox Man, I learned that the elders were right when they taught us:

Doing the right thing isn't always easy.
But doing the right thing is always best.

Dach' qidyuq.
And that is what happened.

dach' qidyuq (dak kwid YOOK): and that is what happened

More About Alaskan Dena'ina Stories

The Dena'ina are an Athabascan language people that, to this day, live in the southern part of Alaska, mostly around Cook Inlet. They are the only Athabascan tribe to have migrated and taken up residence at a coastal location.

The Dena'ina told stories to remind or teach their children how to behave. The stories tell the history of the people and the difficulties they dealt with. They all tell something about Dena'ina culture. The story of *Chia and Fox Man* is about starvation and being orphaned—common problems for the Dena'ina people. It also teaches children about the difficulty of doing the right thing.

Dena'ina homes were often built on hillsides, away from the shoreline. This made surprise attacks from enemies difficult, which was a constant threat for them. Orphans were common as well. Close family would take them in or they would be adopted. If neither option was possible, a wealthy person would take them in as a servant. The chores Chia did in this story are typical of the work everyone had to do. The rich man would have taken Chia in because it was always good to have an extra pair of hands to help out.

Our Uncle Walter told us that starvation, which occurred most often in the late winter or early spring, was one of the most difficult problems the Dena'ina had to deal with.

Like many animals in Dena'ina stories, Fox Man has special powers that enable him to do fantastical things. He is a curious and mysterious figure in Dena'ina lore. This is the only story we know about him.

We used Dena'ina words where appropriate to remind us of the Dena'ina origins of the story, or sukdu. Dena'ina stories throughout time have ended with dach'qidyuk, meaning "and that is what happened…"

Chin'an. Thank you.

Barbara J. and Ethan J. Atwater
Anchorage, Alaska

Dena'ina Glossary

ALASKA

Area where Dena'ina is spoken

Chin'an (chi NUN): Thank you

Dach' qidyuq (dah kwid YOOK): And that is what happened

Di'eshchin (dee USHK een): I am hungry

Dnazeht'in (dnah ZEET een): You stole from me

Duguli (DOO gu lee): Axe

Ezhi'i (ee zhi EE): It is very cold

Sukdu (SOOK du): Story

Qenq'a (KUNK ah): House

Further Reading

Atwater, Barbara J. *Walter's Story: Pedro Bay, Alaska - Past, Present, and Distant Memories.* Anchorage: Publication Consultants, 2012.

Johnson, Walter. James Kari, ed. *I'll Tell You a Story (Sukdu Nel Nuheghelnek): Stories I Recall from Growing up on Iliamna Lake.* Fairbanks: Alaska Native Language Center, University of Alaska Fairbanks, 2004.

Jones, Suzi, James A Fall, and Aaron Leggett, eds. *Dena'inaq' Huch'ulyeshi: The Dena'ina Way of Living.* Fairbanks: Alaska Native Language Center, University of Alaska Fairbanks, 2013.

Kari, James, ed. *Dena'ina topical Dictionary.* Fairbanks: Alaska Native Language Center, University of Alaska Fairbanks, 2013.

Dedication

To our great uncle Walter Johnson who told us many stories, including this one. Whenever he told us a story he would say, "Now you go and tell this story in your own way." We have taken this both as permission and as a directive. Chin'an, thank you, Uncle Walter, for sharing this story with us. We now share it with others.

Thanks also to Gladys Evanoff for her assistance with Dena'ina pronunciations.

Text © 2020 by Barbara J. Atwater and Ethan J. Atwater

Illustrations © 2020 by Mindy Dwyer

Edited by Michelle McCann

Library of Congress Cataloging-in-Publication Data

Names: Atwater, Barbara J., author. | Atwater, Ethan J., author. | Dwyer, Mindy, 1957- illustrator.
Title: Chia and the fox man: an Alaskan Dena'ina fable / retold by Barbara J. Atwater and Ethan J. Atwater; illustrated by Mindy Dwyer.
Description: [Berkeley]: Alaska Northwest Books, [2020] | Includes bibliographical references. | Audience: Ages 5-7. | Audience: Grades K-1. | Summary: "This modern retelling of a traditional Dena'ina story is about Chia, a young boy with a hard life, and his encounter with the legendary Fox Man, who just may be able to help. Through the Fox Man, Chia learns that there is strength in humility and in doing what is right, especially when it's hard."—Provided by publisher.
Identifiers: LCCN 2019037871 (print) | LCCN 2019037872 (ebook) | ISBN 9781513262673 (hardback) | ISBN 9781513262680 (ebook)
Subjects: LCSH: Dena'ina Indians—Folklore. | Indians of North America—Alaska—Folklore. | Foxes—Folklore. | Abandoned children—Mythology—Alaska. | Alaska—Folklore.
Classification: LCC E99.T185 A885 2020 (print) | LCC E99.T185 (ebook) | DDC 398.209798—dc23
LC record available at https://lccn.loc.gov/2019037871
LC ebook record available at https://lccn.loc.gov/2019037872

Printed in China

24 23 22 21 20 1 2 3 4 5

Published by Alaska Northwest Books® an imprint of

WEST MARGIN PRESS

WestMarginPress.com

Proudly distributed by Ingram Publisher Services

WEST MARGIN PRESS
Publishing Director: Jennifer Newens
Marketing Manager: Angela Zbornik
Editor: Olivia Ngai
Design & Production: Rachel Lopez Metzger